STRANGE
MEETINGS

WRITTEN BY **JENNY WAGNER**
ILLUSTRATED BY **IAN FORSS**

Written by Jenny Wagner
Illustrated by Ian Forss
Designed by Christine Deering

Published by Mimosa Publications Pty Ltd
PO Box 779, Hawthorn 3122, Australia
© 1995 Mimosa Publications Pty Ltd
All rights reserved

Literacy 2000 is a Trademark registered in the
United States Patent and Trademark Office.

Distributed in the United States of America by

Rigby
A Division of Reed Elsevier Inc.
500 Coventry Lane
Crystal Lake, IL 60014
800-822-8661

Distributed in Canada by
PRENTICE HALL GINN
1870 Birchmount Road
Scarborough
Ontario M1P 2J7

99 98
10 9 8 7 6 5 4 3
Printed in Hong Kong through Bookbuilders Ltd

ISBN 0 7327 1583 0

CONTENTS

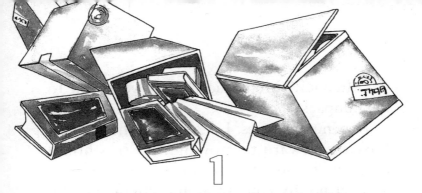

1

MEETING ANITA

Swish-swash! went the princess's broadsword. The cyber-dragons drew back, but only for a moment. Almost at once, they attacked again, and the princess's bronze sword was no match for their steely teeth and armor. "Help me, Michael!" she cried.

Snick-snick! went my slim, supersharp, zenium blade. The cyber-dragons fell clanking to the ground, dropping screws and wires and bits of armor plate ...

"Michael!" said my mother. "Come on, wake up!"

I kept my eyes shut; just one moment more, and the princess would give me my reward. She unclasped her precious gold belt and held it aloft. It glittered in the sun.

"Michael ..."

"Michael!" Mom said. "Don't you want to help unpack?"

I opened my eyes. I did want to help; I was looking forward to moving into this house properly. I wanted to get my room organized, and set up my computer, and check out the neighborhood for people my own age. So I got out of bed.

"Can you remember where you packed our clothes?" said Mom.

Yesterday I'd been so proud of my super packing system that it had seemed a pity to spoil it with labels. So now we had to go through each box in turn, rummaging through books, sheets, toothpaste, talcum powder, and saucepans, in search of some clean clothes to put on.

We looked for ages without finding any. Finally Mom opened a box and dragged out what looked like a blue tent. It was one of my cousin Derek's shirts. Aunt Jean, who hates to waste anything, passes his outgrown clothes on to us, and Mom, who hates to hurt her feelings, takes them.

The only problem is that Derek is built like a Sumo wrestler, while I am built like a weasel.

Mom held the shirt up. "You won't have to wear it for long. It's only till we find your real clothes."

So I put it on, and it was like putting on a swimming pool; a water polo team could have got in there with me. The jeans were just as big. Altogether I looked like Bozo the clown.

Mom, who had found some of Derek's clothes for herself, didn't look any better. But what did it matter? No one was going to see us. We went on unpacking for about an hour, and then the doorbell rang. I forgot how I was dressed, and opened the door without thinking.

A girl was standing there. She was very pretty, in an interesting, careless sort of way – a bit like the princesses I sometimes dreamed about. She even had on a belt that was almost gold-colored. She was holding a casserole dish and staring at me.

"I'm Anita from next door," she said, still staring. Then she added very quickly, "and Mom thought you might like this to save you cooking." She dumped the casserole dish in my hands and fled. I'd made my first impression on the neighborhood.

Mom and I worked steadily all morning, unpacking and putting things away, still without finding our clothes. But I started to get my bedroom organized, which was something, and we had Anita's casserole for lunch.

And when we started unpacking again I found a pleasant surprise. It was a big brown carton like all the others we'd unpacked that day, only this one was brand new, and had NICHOLAS ELECTRONIC INDUSTRIES VECTOR 3e printed on the side.

"A new computer!" I said.

"Don't get too excited," said Mom. "It's only a prototype. There's nothing on it to interest you. That's why I brought it home from the office – to work on some software."

I helped her lift the computer out of its box. It was obviously very advanced. Instead of the usual office-gray color, it was a mean matt black, and it had a row of silver controls, like eyes, along the front. It made my computer look ancient.

"Pretty good, huh?" said Mom. "The other one's in the Westvale office, waiting for someone to come back from vacation. So we're privileged. That's why you have to be super careful not to spill coffee on it."

She said it nicely, but I wished she hadn't reminded me; when my own computer was brand new I left a cup of coffee near it. Someone – surely it wasn't me – knocked it over and blew up the keyboard.

"Another reason for you to be careful," said Mom, trying to cheer me up, "is that it has an infrared modem. Our phone bill's high enough as it is."

The modem sounded interesting. Only the week before, I'd watched a video about a kid with a modem; he hacked into the school computer and changed all his friends' grades to As. Then he nearly destroyed the world, but his mother stopped him in time.

I couldn't help thinking of all the other useful things you could do with a modem – finding friends, for instance.

Mom switched the computer on, grinning like a little girl, and said, "Come on, I'll show you. Your name goes in here ..."

Unfortunately, I didn't see what she was doing, because just then I saw a man coming up our front path, and a moment later the doorbell rang.

Mom went to answer it. I heard a booming voice, and then Mom called from the kitchen, "Michael! There's someone I'd like you to meet."

In the kitchen was a tall, thin man with graying hair and ink stains on his fingers. "This is Mr. Pointright," said Mom. "He's a teacher at the school you'll be going to, and he's just dropped in to say hello."

I was puzzled. No teacher had ever dropped in to say hello to us before. And I wished he'd come when we were properly dressed.

"Hello, Mike," Mr. Pointright said, in the kind of voice that teachers use when they're telling you that you have detention after school.

"It's because Dad's away," Mom said. "Mr. Pointright's a sort of welfare officer."

I didn't like that idea, and I think Mr. Pointright noticed the way I looked. He said, "Your mother needs all the help she can get, Mike. It can't be easy for her, now that she's on her own."

I wanted to say, "Stop talking as though my father's dead or something. He's only away. And one day soon he'll come back, and if he finds you in our kitchen, boy, will *you* be in trouble!"

But I didn't, of course. I just said, "Mom and I are all right."

I did think of showing him Dad's letters, just to see the look on his face. There weren't many – I knew Dad didn't get much chance to write – but they were always lots of fun. Dad was doing secret work for the government. He told me that some of the departments he worked for were so secret that they didn't even have names; they just had initials.

Mr. Pointright gave my hair a playful tug. "All right, Michael. Whatever you say."

When he'd gone, Mom said, "I don't suppose you've found the clothes yet, have you? One of us should go and get some milk."

"I can't!" I said. "Not looking like this." I wasn't too keen on Mom going out looking like that, either, but my instinct for self-preservation was stronger.

"Okay," said Mom, hitching up her Bozo jeans. "I'll get the milk. You take back the casserole dish and go on with the unpacking."

After Mom left, I did another urgent search for some clothes – but I still couldn't find the right boxes. I peered out of the window. There was no sign of anyone next door; maybe I could be quick enough to leave the dish on the front porch and run away before anyone saw me.

I tiptoed up their garden path. So far, so good. There was no one around. I crept over the porch to the door and very, very quietly set the dish down.

I'm sure I didn't make any noise. But just then the door opened, and there was Anita.

She laughed. "I say, I say, I say, it's Bozo!"

I ran back to our house and slammed the door. I'd never been so embarrassed in my life.

Once again, I hunted for our clothes; once again, there was no sign of them. And so, to make myself feel better, and because Mom would be back any minute and I might as well warm it up for her, I sat down in front of the new computer.

2
SWITCHED ON

I didn't even know what I was looking for; a game, perhaps – something to cheer me up. But as soon as I had a proper look at the computer I realized just how advanced it was. Even though it was switched on, I had no idea how to use it. The screen was lit up in a particularly nice shade of blue, but it was completely blank. There wasn't even a prompt.

I pulled the keyboard toward me and tried typing **HELP**. Nothing happened. The letters didn't appear on the screen. I checked that everything was plugged in and tried again. Still nothing. And there wasn't even a mouse.

Six months ago, before I started playing Shadda and The Last Wizard on my own computer, I would simply have given up. But all those months of serious game-playing had left their mark. This was just the Wizard's first gate. I was determined to find a way in.

I stared at the screen and thought hard, as if I hoped it would work by telepathy. It didn't. I ran my fingers over every surface, looking for

VOICE NOT RECOGNIZED

a track-ball, or maybe even another switch. There was still nothing.

"I give up," I said at last.

Success! Well, success of a kind. The computer played a little tune and at last a message appeared on the screen: **VOICE NOT RECOGNIZED. PLEASE REPEAT.**

"I give up," I said.

VOICE NOT RECOGNIZED, said the computer.

"Nice talking to you, too," I muttered.

VOICE NOT RECOGNIZED, said the computer.

Seized by a brighter idea, I said in an imitation of Mom's voice, "I am Rosie Alvarado."

NO YOU ARE NOT, said the computer. **VOICE NOT RECOGNIZED**.

I studied the screen again. It wasn't quite as blank as before; at the top was a button marked VOICE TRAINING. What was that? Did I have to learn to talk in a special way? The idea seemed crazy, but I did the only thing I could think of: I touched the button with my finger.

A new screen came up that really *did* seem crazy:

PLEASE SAY THREE TIMES: CAN THE LADY GET SIMILAR SEEDS FROM IRELAND, OR SHOULD OTHER AWFUL ONES BE SOWN?

"You're joking," I said.

VOICE NOT RECOGNIZED, said the computer.

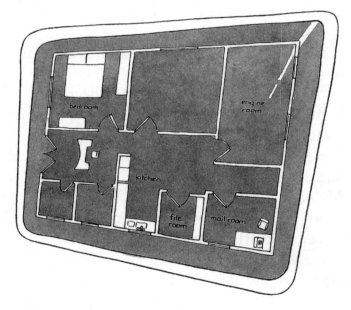

So I did as I was told, and, a fraction of a second later, the plan of a building appeared on the screen.

HELLO, said the computer. **WHERE WOULD YOU LIKE TO WORK? PLEASE CHOOSE A ROOM.**

There was a kitchen, a file room, an engine room, a bedroom, and several others to choose from. But the one I wanted was the little area in the corner with desk and telephone, marked "mailroom."

The computer brought it up for a closer look. There was a memo on the desk for me. It said, **DO YOU WANT TO SEND A MESSAGE?**

I typed "yes." I couldn't believe how easy it suddenly was.

PLEASE TYPE YOUR MESSAGE NOW, said the computer. So I did:

Hello. Is anybody out there? This is Michael, and I'm bored. Please write back, somebody. Goodbye.

I added our phone number and touched a button that said SEND. The computer beeped a warning at me. **YOU HAVE NOT SELECTED A PHONE NUMBER. WHAT NUMBER DO YOU WANT TO SEND TO?**

That was a problem. I didn't know anyone with a modem. So I put in our old number.

There was a pause. Then a message appeared:

THE PHONE NUMBER YOU HAVE ENTERED IS NOT CONNECTED. (C)ANCEL, ENTER ANOTHER OR SELECT (A)UTO.

I didn't know any numbers that *were* connected, so I decided to try the Auto option, whatever that was. Instantly, numbers began flashing onto the screen. Different numbers kept appearing and reappearing for about a minute.

I didn't exactly know what the computer was searching for, but I hoped that it was looking somewhere interesting, like the Seychelles or Greenland, rather than the next suburb.

Then, at last, it gave a jubilant burble, and a long line of numbers settled into place.

My message disappeared from the screen and the words **TRANSMISSION COMPLETE** appeared instead. I'd gotten through to someone!

I hoped that the computer I'd reached wasn't too far away, or that at least it was in a place with a similar time-zone to us. That way I might get a quick answer.

I stared at the screen. Nothing was happening. No one was writing back. But of course it was too early. I had to give them time to read my message and think of something to say. But I couldn't bear the suspense. I went to make a cup of cocoa, so that the time would pass more quickly.

I stayed in the kitchen for exactly ten minutes, which was all I could stand, and when I came back there was a message on the screen:

Hello Michael. I'm bored too. My parents have gone out and I don't think I'm supposed to play with this modem. But I'm so BORED. I live in a house. Do you? Please write back soon - Tania Barton.

I couldn't believe my luck. Not only had I gotten through to someone, but to someone who actually wanted to hear from me.

Admittedly, she sounded a little strange: "I live in a house. Do you?" But that might just mean that she lived somewhere exotic, or in a big city where most people had apartments. Maybe she was incredibly rich and would invite me to visit her mansion. Maybe she had a gold belt and needed rescuing.

I wrote back at once, telling her a bit about myself. I tried to be fairly truthful, but not too truthful; for instance, I didn't really come fourth in the marathon run – it was more like fortieth. But, as Mom always says, it's taking part that counts.

I was about to tell her about my gymnastic leanings, too – well, I once watched the school champion perform on the parallel bars – when I saw Mom's car pulling into the driveway.

I thought she might not like it that I was sitting at the computer having fun while there was still so much to unpack, so I finished my letter at racing speed:

Habve to go now. Why don't you write bavk tonotrow? - M

And I quickly added:

P.S. Don't take too much notice of what I said about the marathon.

Then I hit "exit."

That night, Mom worked until very late. I lay in bed listening to the soft tap, tap of the keys, and the rise and fall of her voice as she talked to the computer.

I felt very pleased with myself. I'd found my way into a computer that thought it worked for the CIA, and I'd found a new friend as well, which was the best thing. Not only that, but I'd been particularly careful about leaving the computer as I'd found it. I'd deleted everything I'd done.

Oh no. *Everything?*

Every single word.

I'd deleted it all, including Tania's phone number.

3
MY HERO!

The first thought I had in the morning was that I'd deleted the most interesting piece of knowledge I'd ever had in my whole life; the second thought was the same as the first, all over again.

I spent the morning doing more unpacking – the piles of boxes were gradually getting smaller, but our clothes still hadn't turned up, so once again I had to wear a Bozo outfit.

I kept thinking about Tania and wondering whether she still had my phone number – and how I would ever manage to get in touch with her again if she hadn't. What if she'd been as careful about cleaning up as I'd been – and just deleted me?

At lunchtime, Mom went out to get some pizza – a reward for us both because we'd worked so hard. And because I needed a rest after all that hard work, I switched the computer on again.

I needn't have worried about Tania. There was a message waiting on the mail desk for me.

Hello Michael, I really liked your letter, and it's all right; I didn't really believe you were a famous athlete. I'm not either, how's that? But I like running and I came tenth in the sprint.

I have to be careful using this computer. Dad brought it home from work. He said that it's a special one and that there are only two like it in the world. So I'm not supposed to use it but I'm not exactly using the computer, am I? Not just the computer. Really I'm using the modem. Apparently it's the modem that's really special - it's a sort of infrared one.

I'm bored because we only just moved here and I don't know anybody and I'm not allowed out much. Please write back as soon as you can. - Tania.

My pulse rate suddenly quickened. A princess imprisoned in a tower! I glanced back over the earlier part of her letter, where she talked about the modem. It seemed too close to be mere coincidence. Could Tania be using

the other computer, the mate to this one? Maybe whoever it was had come back from their vacation. I didn't understand how a modem might seek its mate, but that could explain why I'd found Tania so easily.

There was something else to think about. If Tania was using the other computer, that meant that she must live in Westvale. It wasn't as exciting as Greenland, but at least it would make her accessible. Westvale was only two suburbs away.

I wrote back:

Tania, what does your computer look like?

She answered: **Like a computer. Maybe a bit strange looking. A bit black. A bit big ... Why?**

I wrote: **Look on the left side of the case. Is there a brand name? And what is it?**

Within seconds her answer came back:

It says Vector 3e. Are you going to tell me why you want to know?

Tania, I wrote, **you'll never believe this. We're using twin computers. I'm using a Vector 3e, too. And my Mom brought it home from work, too! Isn't that an amazing coincidence? How was your day? Mine was OK. I've got a lot of work to do. I should be doing it now - only this is more fun. - M**

Then Tania's reply gave me even more to think about:

That's really weird about the two computers. Are they linked to each other or what? But it might be useful because there's a problem with this one. Does yours have any spare bits with it? One reason I'm not allowed to use this one is that a part is faulty and it's

getting worse. Your messages keep breaking up and the only way I can read them is with Decode. Soon it'll be too bad even for that. - T

She *did* need rescuing! I wrote back at once: What part? I'll help if I can. - M

It turned out to be something so ordinary that at first I thought she was joking. It was a cable: an ordinary, flat, gray ribbon cable. I was about to write back to her and say, "You can get one at any electronics store," when I realized what she was *really* saying.

Obviously she had damaged the cable in some way and couldn't tell her parents; when the cable finally gave up she'd be in big trouble – not to mention not being able to communicate with me anymore. No wonder she was asking for my help! So I wrote:

Don't worry. It's just a cable. I'll get one for you tomorrow. - M

I thought that her answer was a bit over the top, but I couldn't help feeling flattered:

Oh, Michael! Can you really do that? That would be so fantastic! I live at 17 Utah St. Westvale, just opposite the park entrance, only don't meet me there. Meet me in the park, in the coffee shop, and then I can buy you a cup of coffee. Is 4 o'clock OK? Thank

you, thank you, my hero! You can recognize me easily because I'm small and have dark hair and I'll be wearing a gold belt. - T

My good luck was unbelievable! Just in case it didn't last, I sent a quick note back, agreeing to the time and the place, and signed off.

This time I was more careful. I made multiple copies of her address and phone number, on disk and on paper. I could barely keep from singing as I wrote it all down in my diary and at the back of my homework book; I don't think I'd ever been so happy in my life.

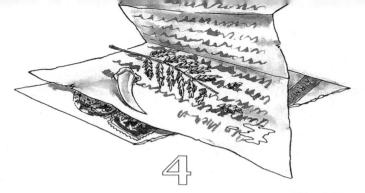

4

A CABLE AND A ROSE

"Guess what?" said Mom at breakfast next morning. "There's a letter from Dad." And she handed it to me.

There was a mystery about these letters that I could never figure out. A letter for me never came in its own envelope, with a foreign postmark and stamp, as you might expect. Instead, they were always enclosed in Mom's letters. Once I asked her why Dad never sent me a proper letter where I could have the stamps, and she said, "He goes to some very remote places. It's hard enough for him to send a letter at all. Two envelopes and stamps would be too much."

But it didn't sound right to me. In that case, why didn't Mom give me the stamps from her letters? But I never even saw the envelopes, and she never showed me her letters, even when I showed her mine.

This letter was shorter than usual, and it didn't help to solve the mystery:

Dear Mike,

Button your rollerblades and keep your hat on! Here comes a letter from your old Dad, who has spent the last week battling alligators in a Venezuelan swamp, and wasn't sure if he'd get out to tell the tale.

As you see, we were lucky. However, my assistant had the misfortune to come out minus a leg, and we lost much valuable time in looking for it and having it reattached. Fortunately it is now as good as new, although his alligator shoes don't quite match - due to an oversight, I think. They came from different alligators.

The secret project I am involved in has hit a few snags, I'm afraid, so I may not be home for your birthday as I'd hoped.. But some time, when I'm near civilization, I'll send you a present, and I'll write whenever I can. I'm sorry I can't give you an address to write back to, or even a phone number. I have to keep moving, you see, or the alligators will catch up.

Lots of love, and keep your chin up,

Dad.

A letter from Dad should have made me happy, and of course it did, but I hated not being able to write back. I wanted to tell him it was all right if he couldn't make it for my birthday. I'd be okay, and I didn't want him to take any stupid risks.

I wanted to tell him I was looking forward to his secret assignment being over so he could come home – but, if I had to, I could wait as long as necessary.

"We don't have to wear Derek's clothes today," said Mom. "I washed the clothes we arrived in, and they're dry."

I was pleased to hear that, because this morning I had to go out and buy Tania's cable, and I didn't think I could do it dressed like Bozo; there were some things I couldn't do even for a princess.

So I got dressed in proper clothes and emptied my money box. I hoped that I'd have enough to pay for the cable and to big-note myself as well. Even though Tania had offered to pay for the coffee, I wanted to say in a masterful kind of way, and if possible in a deep voice, "No, no, Tania, I'll take care of it."

But I didn't even get as far as Utah Street before I ran into trouble. At the electronics store on the corner, I discovered that the short length of ribbon cable I wanted would cost a whole 31 dollars: 17 dollars for the cable itself, and seven dollars each for the little metal connectors on each end.

This was stretching my resources, but I knew that, with any luck, I'd get it back. I was sure Tania would insist on paying for the cable. I'd let her offer twice, and then, the third time, I'd say with a great show of reluctance, "Oh, all right, since you *insist*." But there was no way I was going to ask her for money. You don't rescue a princess from a tower and then hand her the bill.

I unwrapped the cable from its dull gray packet and bought a gift box for it; and then, on a sudden impulse, I spent all my left-over money on a single red rose to go on top. As soon as I found out where in the coffee shop Tania was sitting, I was going to sneak up and silently lay the box and its rose in front of her – and hope she meant it when she said she'd pay for the coffee.

But as I walked down Utah Street I began to wonder if I'd made a mistake. The street was full of auto-electricians, radiator repair shops, and spare-parts dealers; the only park I could see was a vacant lot that was being used as a car park; it was shaded by the brick wall of the car wash next door. There wasn't a private house in sight, and certainly not one that a princess might live in.

I cheered myself up with the thought that Utah Street was quite long. Maybe at the other end it was different. In any case, I was at the wrong end of the street – number 17 would have to be right at the other end.

But as I walked on, my misgivings grew. There was one commercial building after another: a knitwear factory, an umbrella warehouse, a wine and vinegar merchant. I got almost to the other end of Utah Street, and there was still no sign of either a park or a private house. Number 17 turned out to be a furniture mover's warehouse.

I wondered if I'd misread Tania's message; perhaps she'd written "Utan Street" or "Ulan Street" or something like that. I walked back the way I'd come; my disappointment was so strong I could taste it.

At the warehouse I saw a rumpled-looking woman coming down the steps, and with a last glimmer of hope I asked if she knew whether there were any streets in the area that had similar names. She looked as if she was in a hurry, but something in my appearance seemed to arouse her good nature – I must have looked pathetic with my gold box, my single rose, and my downturned mouth. She thought for a few moments and even went back into the warehouse office to ask if anyone else had any ideas.

But the answer was no. It was Utah Street or nothing.

I tried to say thanks, but tears were pricking my eyelids, and my throat seemed to be full of wet socks, so all the woman got from me was a bleak nod and an even more downcast expression than before.

When I got home, my first instinct was to throw everything in the garbage, where I'd never have to look at it again. But I'm too much of an optimist. Just in case one day another princess needed a ribbon cable, I thought it might be useful to have one. So I left the rose on the kitchen counter as a present for Mom, and put the box and cable at the bottom of a cupboard.

I couldn't believe that Tania, of all people, would play such a trick on me. She'd seemed so nice! A little too nice, perhaps, looking back. Now that I thought about it, that last message of hers, the one that was so flattering and extravagant, seemed suspicious; how could anyone get so excited over a bit of cable? But I'd been so desperate to believe her that I'd swallowed every word.

Mom had gone into the office and was going to be late, so I warmed up a frozen something for dinner. (I discovered afterwards that it was brains and broccoli, but luckily at the time I was too distracted to notice.) Then I went to bed.

I couldn't get to sleep. As I lay there staring at the ceiling I couldn't get the questions out of my mind. Why did Tania do it? What had I ever done to her?

Before long, an answer occurred to me. She'd said that she was small and had dark hair. That sounded just like ... And, I suddenly realized, she had almost the same name.

Rearrange the letters of Tania, and you get ... Anita.

I felt sick.

5
DEAR MIKE ...

The next morning, Mom suggested that we go for a walk together to explore the new neighborhood, but I just wasn't in the mood. So she decided to spend some time on the computer, and I went off to finish fixing up my room.

I thought I might as well do a good job of it, so I did something I wouldn't normally do – I started rummaging about in the cleaning cupboard. I wanted something to clean my windows with. But as I scrabbled away among bottles of bath cleaner and floor polish, I came across something else. Hidden at the back of the cupboard, under a neat pile of yellow polishing cloths, I found a wooden box – a deed box.

I am a sucker for wooden boxes of any kind, but especially deed boxes. When you see them in movies they always contain important documents that reveal amazing secrets.

And so did this one. When I lifted the lid and peered inside, I saw that it was full of letters. But not any old letters.

These were new letters, and they were addressed to me. They were in plain white envelopes with "Michael" written on the front in my father's handwriting, and where the stamp should have been there was a date.

They were all arranged in order, from the earliest to the latest. The first one, I noticed, was dated only two weeks away – on my birthday. And since it was addressed to me, I opened it.

Dear Mike,

Here's another letter from your old dad, just to wish you a very happy birthday and say I'm sorry I can't be there. I really had hoped to, but on the way back from Venezuela I had to take a detour through the Himalayas, and my assistant dropped one of his alligator shoes in a crevasse. Fortunately his leg was not attached to it, and so we were able to ...

I put the letter down and looked at another, dated a month later. Then another, two weeks later still. They were the same sort of letters that I always got, full of exciting stories of great adventures and hairsbreadth escapes. I knew that Dad loved exaggerating, and I knew that his work was so top secret that he couldn't really tell me all the real details of his work ... but *none* of it was real. It was all made up, all a fraud. Mom was handing out these letters on the due dates, just to keep me happy.

So where was Dad? And why couldn't he send me the letters himself?

It took awhile for it to sink in, but at last the obvious answer occurred to me: where is it you are kept against your will and not allowed to post letters?

In jail, of course.

So that was it. My dad was a jailbird. Yes, he was working for the government all right; he was sewing mailbags and making license plates.

Now I understood about Mr. Pointright. Mom had called him "a sort of a welfare

officer," and now I knew what sort. He was the sort who keeps an eye on families like ours – families whose father is in jail. I knew I'd never be able to look him in the eye again.

I forgot about cleaning my windows. I went back to my room and caught up with Shadda and The Last Wizard instead, and pushed any thoughts about Anita, Tania, or my father right to the back of my mind.

But in the afternoon Mom came to my room and said, "You're unusually quiet today. Anything on your mind?"

"No," I muttered. "Should there be?"

Mom shrugged. "That's what I was asking you." I was afraid that she would ask more questions, but she just glanced at my computer game winking away in the corner – I'd just reached Gate 7 and it was anxious to move on – and said, "I thought you might like to watch a video with me tonight. And something easy for dinner. Spaghetti?"

"Fantastic!"

My enthusiasm might have seemed a bit overdone, but there were good reasons. Watching a good movie with Mom probably would help to cheer me up a bit, but I'd thought of something else, too. It would take Mom awhile to join up at a local video store, so I'd have the privacy I needed to grit my teeth and get back to the computer.

No, I wasn't going to get in touch with Tania. At least, that wasn't my intention to begin with. To get my mind off things, I was going to investigate some of the 3e's other functions. But then I had a better idea: I *would* send a message. I started typing:

Dear Tania,

Sorry I didn't turn up for coffee. There didn't seem to be much point because I didn't get the cable. I was so busy enjoying myself with my friends that I forgot about it. - M

Nyah, nyah, nyah! I thought, and I was about to press "send" when the computer beeped and a box appeared, superimposed on the screen: **URGENT MESSAGE FOLLOWS**.

And a second later the urgent message appeared. It said,(¬__*!7ᴙs2()_{ 421Ñ #{. ø_/-}_ _{|, ~_°8."

I stared at it. I searched for a decode button. Nothing. Then I wondered if "Tania" had been partly telling the truth; maybe there really was a problem with her cable. In that case, since this computer was a twin to hers, I could expect a problem with this cable, too.

The thought made me feel unexpectedly happy. It looked as if I hadn't wasted my money on the cable after all. I got it out of its box and then called up the menu screen again. What room in the building would give me access to the computer's internal workings?

"Engine room," I said.

The screen that came up was totally incomprehensible. It was full of strange lines, squiggles, symbols, and arrow-like things pointing in all directions, and none of them made sense.

"Help," I said.

WHAT SORT OF HELP DO YOU REQUIRE? said the computer.

That was the problem; I didn't even know enough to know what sort of help to ask for. I sat there pondering, not knowing what to do, until I saw the flash of headlights and Mom's car pulled into the driveway.

I didn't want to explain to her what I'd been doing with the computer; I was afraid I might end up telling her all about my humiliation. So I started to exit. But at the last moment, I looked again at the urgent message. It seemed a shame to delete it before I knew what it said. So I printed it.

As Mom came in, I noticed that the cable was still lying on top of the computer where I'd left it. But I couldn't tell her about the faulty cable without telling her the rest of the story, so I said nothing and hoped she wouldn't notice.

The next morning, while Mom and I were getting breakfast ready, she said, "I thought I told you to be careful with the new computer."

"I have been," I said.

Mom shook her head, reached into a cupboard, and took out a blue and white cup. "Then what was this doing on it this morning?"

"I don't know. I only got out of bed a few minutes ago."

"It was full of coffee – cold coffee, so it had been there awhile. Do you know how much damage you might have done if you'd knocked it over?"

"Yes," I said. "But it wasn't me."

Mom wasn't listening. "It wouldn't be the first time, would it?"

"No," I mumbled.

Mom hates to catch herself nagging. "Well, I don't want to push the point. Just don't do it again, okay?" She looked at the cup. "It's rather pretty. Where did you get it?"

I supposed it must have been in the house when we came. I'd certainly never seen it before, and I had no idea how it had got onto the computer. Maybe Mom had left it there herself; she gets a bit vague when she's working, though she'd never admit it.

I was back to wearing Bozo clothes again because my one set of ordinary clothes was in the wash. Mom and I had continued our search – and she'd even called the moving company to see if they'd accidentally kept some of our boxes – but there was no sign of our proper clothes yet.

Finally Mom said, "This is ridiculous. I'm going out to buy some more."

I was horrified. "I can't go with you! Suppose I meet someone I know!" The only person I knew in this neighborhood was Anita, but that was enough.

"Okay," said Mom, picking up her car keys. She grinned. "As long as I can choose what to buy you. How about some tartan flares?" She was out the door before I realized what she'd said. I opened the door and yelled, "Over my dead body!"

The new cable was still on the computer where I'd left it, and I thought I might try once again to run a test on the old one. But then the blank screen reminded me that I had a score to settle with Anita. It wouldn't hurt to do that first.

The insulting message I'd been going to send her had been wiped when I turned the computer off last night. But it was no trouble to write another.

Dear Tania, Sorry I didn't turn up

At that moment, something made me look at the cable again. One end had slipped down over the front of the computer, and the connector was almost touching one of the silver buttons.

As I reached up to push it back, the movement of my hand must have caused a slight breeze. The end of the cable brushed against the button. And a window appeared on the screen:

TRANSFER ENABLED. DO YOU WISH TO CONTINUE? (Y)ES (R)ESET (C)ANCEL

I didn't know what it meant, so I decided that the letter could wait. But I was curious. "Yes," I said.

Out of the corner of my eye I saw a small, silent red flash. Then there was nothing. I mean nothing.

The cable wasn't there anymore.

6

WHERE AM I?

I stared stupidly at the place where the cable had been. What had I done? Had there been a short circuit? And had it released so much energy that I'd vaporized an entire cable? If so, what had I done to the computer's insides?

And what would Mom do to me?

I looked behind the computer and around it, in the faint hope that maybe I'd just imagined the red flash and the cable had fallen down by itself. But there was no sign of it anywhere. And another unexpected thing had happened; somehow or other, the short had caused my half-finished message to be sent. The words "Sorry I didn't turn up" had disappeared, and in their place were the words **TRANSMISSION COMPLETE.** Great. Now Anita would think I was apologizing to her.

It was time to leave the computer alone. In fact, now I was wishing I'd never touched it. I exited in a hurry, erasing my changes as usual, only this time I had a strong urge to wipe off my fingerprints as well.

I thought Mom would be much happier if she came home and saw that the unpacking was nearly finished, so I spent some time trying to make the living room look neat and welcoming, instead of it looking like a junkyard. But I was so nervous about what I might have done to the computer that I couldn't concentrate.

In the end, I decided I had to find out; it was better than waiting for Mom to come home and find out for me. So I switched the computer on.

To my relief, everything seemed normal. Cautiously I called up the mailroom. That was okay, too. There was even a message for me:

Dear Michael,

Thank you for the cable! And for saying you were sorry. I can read your messages better now. - Tania.

I thought she was being sarcastic, although I couldn't really be sure. But there was certainly something strange going on. I peered at the buttons along the front. They were labeled DIAGNOSTICS, TRANSFER, RESET and POST.

"Post?" Post as in "post office?" My stomach suddenly knotted. I knew this was an ultra-modern computer, but could it actually have mailed the cable somewhere? It didn't seem possible. And yet …

I could have tested my hypothesis by pressing the POST button and waiting to see what happened. But I wasn't brave enough. Instead I called up the help screen.

WHAT WOULD YOU LIKE HELP WITH, MICHAEL? it asked.

I said, with a slight quaver in my voice, "Post."

POST = POWER ON SELF TEST, said the computer. **DO YOU WISH TO CONTINUE?**

"Yes," I said, holding my breath.

The computer burbled a tune, and messages flashed on the screen: **SELF TEST IN PROGRESS**, then **SELF TEST COMPLETE. OK. INTERMITTENT FAULT IN CABLE UJB36L**

Of course. Power On Self Test. What else would POST stand for? The computer had tested a cable in its inner works and found an intermittent fault. But I'd already suspected that. Grateful that no one had been watching, and even more grateful that the computer was still working, I called up the mailroom again and started another letter.

Dear Tania

Just then I heard Mom's car. I was just about to exit when I noticed that there was a mark on one of the silver buttons. Hoping that it was just dust, I rubbed it with my finger. A window appeared on the screen:

TRANSFER ENABLED. DO YOU WISH TO CONTINUE? (Y)ES (R)ESET (C)ANCEL

I didn't know what to do. I just wanted to exit, and in a hurry. How was I going to get out of this screen?

Mom appeared in the doorway, carrying shopping bags.

"Do you want to try on your new jeans?"

"Thanks, that'd be great!" I called back.

"What did you say?"

"Thanks! Yes!" I yelled.

"I have to take the …"

I never found out what it was she had to take. Maybe "yes" hadn't actually been the best thing to say; almost at once, I felt a draft of warm, dry air round my fingers, and the hair on my knuckles stood up. Then there was a silent red flash, and the lights went out.

I kept quite still, afraid to move in case I bumped into something. Then my eyes got used to the darkness and I realized that the lights hadn't gone out; they'd simply dimmed. Whatever had made the red flash must have caused a voltage drop.

Then I remembered. The lights weren't even on. This was midafternoon. It was still broad daylight – or it should have been.

I looked at the rug I was standing on. I looked at it very carefully; it was a red and blue patterned Persian rug and I'd never seen it before. We didn't have a Persian rug in our house.

Nor did we have a glass-fronted bookcase, a black leather armchair, a clear plastic telephone with all its works showing, or any of the other things that were in the room.

I was in someone else's house.

7
MEETING TANIA

The light was dim because the blinds were drawn. But the blinds didn't fit the windows exactly, and sunlight was leaking in around the edges. There was enough light to see that the room I was in was small with white walls. And it was full of odd turns and corners, nothing like the square, pink rooms at our place.

And whoever this room belonged to had strange taste in decoration: it was a bizarre mixture of luxury and seediness. There was an opulent Persian rug on the floor, but worn-out slatted blinds on the windows; ornate light fittings hung from the ceiling, but the furniture hadn't been looked after – even though it was nearly new, it was covered in dents and scratches.

Next to the window there was a small table with a number of objects displayed on it. There was a faded wooden ruler marked in inches and centimeters; a frayed tape measure marked the same way; a scratched green mug full of pencils and pens, and an ordinary milk carton with a bunch of yellow plastic roses in it.

I tried to remember how I'd got here. I knew that something bad had happened to me, but what? Maybe I'd hit my head on something and I'd come to this house for help. But whose house was it? And why had I chosen it?

But then I turned around, and there, standing on a scuffed white desk, was a familiar computer – the twin to Mom's black Vector 3e. I was so relieved I laughed out loud. Maybe I didn't know how I got here, but at least now I knew where I was. I was in Tania's house!

Someone must have heard me laughing. There was a movement outside, and then the door opened and a girl came in.

At first I thought it was Anita; she had the same hair and the same pretty features. But this girl was dressed in a way that Anita would never even imagine: she looked like Mrs. Bozo. She was wearing the baggiest jeans I'd ever seen, and her huge brown and white shirt looked like my granddad's pajama top.

"Tania?" I said. I cleared my throat. "I'm Michael."

"So that's what you look like! I love your shirt; it's disgusting. How did you get in?"

Before I could answer, she went on breathlessly, "Thanks again and again for the cable. Do you want a drink or something? The reason I'm talking so much is that I'm nervous about meeting you. It's amazing that you got in!"

I could hardly tell her I was amazed about it myself, so I said nothing, and instead showed a deep interest in the table with its display of junk.

"It's pretty, isn't it?" said Tania. "That's my mother's doing. She has an artistic streak – she makes these pretty little corners all over the house. Anyway, however you got in, it's comprehensively disgusting!"

There was an admiring note in her voice, so I wasn't offended by her words, but I was puzzled by her air of astonishment. It's true I couldn't remember how I got into the house, but I thought it was probably in the usual way – by walking in through the door. Tania seemed to think that I'd tunneled in under the foundations.

"We keep the blinds shut in the afternoons to keep the sun off things, but it's okay now." She gave the cord a gentle tug and the blind opened, giving me a view of the garden.

I think that was when I began at last to understand; at least, I realized then why Tania was so surprised I'd got in. The house was a fortress. Steel bars guarded the windows, and around the leafy garden there was a high brick wall topped with broken glass. The garden was deeply shaded, and where the shadows were thickest I could see random flashes of light, like glowworms; they looked like pulses from some sort of surveillance equipment.

"Where are the dogs?" I said, trying to sound cool. "And the armed guards?"

"In the kitchen. It's their coffee break."

I decided she was probably joking.

"I was a bit chizzed when you didn't turn up for coffee," Tania said. "That's why I didn't write for awhile. But then I came in here at lunchtime and there was the cable. And it works! You must've been hiding in the house all this time. So how did you get in? No, you'd better not say. I wouldn't want you to get into trouble."

No, I thought, looking out at the fortified garden. I wouldn't want to get into trouble, either. Not here.

"This is Mom's office," said Tania. "I'm allowed to work in here, as long as I don't touch the computer. So you can hide in here if you like."

"Hide? Why should I hide?"

Tania looked at me as if I'd asked why I should wear clothes. "Because you're not invited."

"So invite me."

"How can I? You're already here."

It was becoming obvious that my first guess about Tania had been right. She really *was* strange.

In fact, the whole situation – this odd room, the anti-invasion precautions outside, and the bizarre way I'd gotten here – was making me more and more uncomfortable. Tania was friendly enough, and it was interesting to meet her, but now more than anything I wanted to go home.

I moved over to the computer – it looked exactly like the one at home, which made me

feel a little more comfortable. Wanting to get
away, but hoping to sound smooth and in

control, I said, "Well then, I'll be going. See you later. Glad you liked the cable."

Tania led the way and I followed her into a wide entrance hall. "How will you get out?" she said.

The entrance hall seemed to have been decorated by the same person who decorated the office. Oriental rugs of various sizes were layered all over the floor like in an Arabian tent, and the walls were hung with framed pictures.

But the pictures weren't the grand sort I would have expected to see in a house like this; they were simply faded color photographs of jumbo jets. The series was called "The Golden Age of Aviation."

There was something vaguely familiar about the way the pictures were framed, but I had to think for a few minutes before I realized what it was: my grandmother had a picture of a sailing ship that was framed in the same style. Hers was called "The Golden Age of Sail."

"Go on," said Tania impatiently. "Do your stuff. I want to see how you get out."

At first I didn't know what she meant. I stood there looking around the entrance hall, examining each wall in turn. I was all ready to walk out of there, except for one problem. There was no door. Well, there was something that might have been a door. Or it might have been a mirror. Set into one of the walls was a large, smooth rectangle of shiny metal, with no knob, no handle, no latch, and no lock.

"Well?" said Tania.

"Well what?"

"Tell it your name."

I didn't turn a hair. I was getting used to talking to inanimate objects. "Michael Alvarado," I said. Nothing happened.

"Try again," said Tania.

I did. Still nothing happened.

"It doesn't recognize you," she said. "That's because you're not on the invited guest list. Are you going to try again?"

"Should I?"

"It's up to you."

I knew from playing chess with my father that when someone says "It's up to you," like that, it means you'd better not.

I said, "What happens if I do?"

"The door will call the security guards and they'll take you away." She grinned at me. "So, now would you like me to hide you?"

I thought that was a wonderful idea.

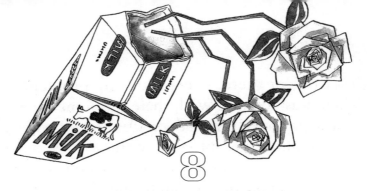

8

STRANDED

It was nice of Tania to hide me, but I would definitely have preferred to go home. It was getting late. A soft twilight was settling on the garden; in the office, without my noticing it, the lighting had come on.

"Tania," I said, "just how long were you thinking of hiding me for?"

"As long as it's necessary. Don't worry, you're safe while you're with me." She was grinning again; I had the feeling she was teasing me.

"Couldn't I just talk to your Mom and Dad?" I hadn't worked out what I was going to say to them, but I was sure they couldn't keep me here if I didn't want to stay.

"They're not home from work yet."

I gazed at the deepening twilight outside. This time of day always made me feel as if I should be going home. I thought of our warm kitchen at home, and the smell of potatoes cooking; I wondered if Mom had actually seen me disappear, or if she had even noticed I was missing, and whether she was worried about me.

And in between, I was still worrying about how I'd gotten into this fortress of a house. After seeing the bars on the windows I knew I couldn't have gotten in that way. And I couldn't have come in through the front door, or it would have let me out again.

That didn't leave many choices. Especially when I considered something else: I wasn't the only thing that had turned up like a ghost, without going through doors. There was also the cable.

I had to face up to it: I had gotten here the same way. I didn't like the idea, but it had one thing in its favor: at least now I could go home. All I had to do was reverse the process.

Tania saw me looking at the computer. She was silent for awhile, then she said, "That's how you got here, isn't it? I wondered." She took a large red and white spotted handkerchief from her pocket and blew her nose; I thought the clown handkerchief went well with her baggy jeans. She paused for a moment, twisting the handkerchief in her fingers, and then she said, "I wasn't going to mention this – I didn't know how you'd take it. But I think I sent you a cup of coffee today."

So that's where it came from! "Yes, my Mom got it. Thanks."

"It was an accident. I put it down on the computer and there was a red flash, and it was gone." She switched the computer on and asked for the mailroom. "I suppose you'll want to go home now."

"It is getting late." Then I said, "Maybe I'll come again. But by bus next time."

"Okay."

I took up my position in front of the computer and pressed the transfer button. The screen came up and I entered our home number. The window appeared as before:

TRANSFER ENABLED. DO YOU WISH TO CONTINUE?

"Thanks for hiding me," I said to Tania, and gave her a little wave. "Yes," I said to the computer.

"Bye," said Tania, waving back.

I waited for the warm, dry air blowing around my fingers, and the silent red flash.

Nothing happened. Instead, a message appeared on the screen:

REMOTE IS NOT RESPONDING. REDIALING.

The computer redialed again and again, but still nothing happened. And then I remembered. What was Mom saying just as I left? "I have to take the ..."

Of course. She'd had to take the computer back. I tried her number at work.

The computer replied, **THE PHONE NUMBER YOU HAVE ENTERED IS NOT CONNECTED. (C)ANCEL OR ENTER ANOTHER.**

I tried again, and got the same message. Then I tried the number of the Westvale office, and got the message again.

"Anything wrong?" said Tania.

"I don't know," I said. "I suppose it means I'll have to go home the slow way – when your parents let me out of here. What time do they get home?"

"Not for ages. They always work late on Thursdays."

I thought that was an odd thing to say, especially since it was Monday, but a lot of things Tania said didn't quite make sense, and I was getting used to it. I thought it was just her way – she liked to say crazy things as a joke, I supposed. So I let it pass.

In any case, when you've said all your goodbyes and made all your promises to keep in touch, it's embarrassing when you can't go after all. So I looked around the room, counted the knots on the blind cord, and then, because there was a gaping silence and I felt obliged to fill it, I said, "So what did your parents do to need a house like this? Work for The Mob, or what?"

I was sorry as soon as I'd said it. With my own father in jail, I was hardly in a position to be smart about someone else's.

Tania was immediately offended. "The house is full of antiques," she said stiffly. "Mom and Dad are afraid of getting burgled. And do

you mind," she nodded at the scuffed black leather chair I was flopped in, "not sprawling in that chair? It's an antique."

I knew it was nothing of the kind – our school principal had one that was very similar, only better looked after – but I sat up straight and tried to think of something polite to say that would restore the good mood between us.

I remembered that, in an early letter, Tania said her parents had brought their computer home from work. So I said chattily, "Did you know that your parents and my Mom work for the same people?"

She looked surprised. "How could that be?"

"They all work for Nicholas Electronic Industries. My mom works in Beckersby, and your mom and dad work in the Westvale office."

"What Westvale office? Mom and Dad don't work for anyone. They have an antique shop in the Supermall."

We were getting into one of Tania's muddy conversations again. If I wasn't careful I would say something like, "What do you mean, the Supermall?" and she would answer, "The place where my parents' shop is."

So I said, "An antique shop? Didn't your parents bring your computer home from work?"

"Yes," Tania said patiently. "They brought it home from their antique shop. What's wrong with that? It's an antique."

I wanted to yell at her. I wanted to shout, "Don't be stupid! How can a computer like this be an antique?" But the truth was, I already knew. I remembered what she'd said a few minutes ago, about her parents working late on Thursdays. I'd chosen not to make a fuss about it then, but now I said, "You know very well it's Monday!"

She blinked at me. "It's Thursday. That's why my parents are late and why the house security is minding me."

I found myself shaking, gently at first, but then more and more violently. If, in traveling from my place to Tania's, I'd skipped two days, how did I know that I hadn't skipped more? How did I know that I hadn't skipped months, or even years?

I had to know. "Tania," I said, "what year is this?"

And she told me. I had jumped into the future by eighty years.

The news was shocking enough, but seconds later the implications sank in. If the computer had been moved, then I had no way of getting home. And, anyway, I probably had no home to go to. Mom, Dad, my friends, even the irritating Mr. Pointright, were all either very, very old or dead.

Convulsively, I gripped the antique milk carton. When I looked again, I had squeezed it to the size of a tennis ball.

9
LOST IN
TRANSMISSION

I think maybe Tania felt sorry for me. Out of kindness to my feelings, she didn't mention the age of the milk carton, or even how valuable it had been.

Instead, she took me into the kitchen and made a cup of coffee. It tasted nothing like coffee – it was thick and syrupy – but it was a hot drink, and there was some comfort in that. I didn't mind the kitchen, either. It had a sort of familiar look, like a kitchen I'd seen in a movie or a sitcom.

Tania saw me looking around. "I know," she said. "I wish Mom and Dad would fix up this kitchen so that it wasn't so antique. I'm always embarrassed in front of my friends. Living in an old house is bad enough."

"It's fine," I said. "It makes me feel at home."

Tania sat down at the kitchen counter and switched on what seemed to be a computer. I caught a glimpse of a three dimensional color picture, and quickly turned my back; I didn't like being reminded of where – or rather, when – I was, and I felt safer with the kitchen's more old-fashioned features.

"I've got an idea," said Tania. "According to my parents, there's another of these Vector 3e computers around somewhere. Maybe we can check with the library and find out where it was in your day."

Of course this wasn't the twin of Mom's computer. This was the *same* computer, only it was now eighty years old. "Would the library know?" I said. "Computers are pretty common things in my day. Libraries don't usually keep track of them."

"But it must have been a pretty famous computer in its time. Look at what it can do."

I thought about that, and decided there was a problem with Tania's argument. For some reason, the computer wasn't commonplace in Tania's time. Even Tania's parents, who would have known a lot about antiques, seemed to know hardly anything about this one.

Otherwise they wouldn't have let her anywhere near it.

So why hadn't the computer survived into Tania's time? It seemed that the Vector 3e hadn't gone into production after all. I wondered why, and a possible answer came almost at once. Maybe it didn't work properly. So what might we find if we looked up old newspapers?

Unfortunately, I could just imagine:

BOY VAPORIZED BY PROTOTYPE COMPUTER
Mother powerless to help

MOM SEES BOY ZAPPED
"He never had a chance" says weeping mom

KIDNAPPED!!
ROGUE COMPUTER SNATCHES BOY

COMPUTER BOY – DAY 3
Ransom note expected soon

COMPUTER BOY'S MEMORIAL SERVICE
Hopes fade for plucky youngster

"Tania," I said, "do we have to go to the library?"

"There's nothing on the ultranet," said Tania, after awhile, "so I guess we'll have to."

"I can't get out of the house, remember?" I was so glad of the excuse that I couldn't keep the smugness out of my voice. I wasn't just afraid of what I might discover in the library; since learning that what was out there wasn't my real world, I wanted to stay as far away from it as possible.

And there was just a chance that if I kept trying Mom's work number, eventually the modem might be attached to it.

"You can go through the door if I'm with you," said Tania. "It's just that we won't be able to get in again. Not till Mom and Dad come home."

I didn't like that idea, either. It was bad enough having to leave the familiar surroundings of the house, without being trapped in the alien environment outside. "Can't you go to the library without me?" I said. "I'll be fine by myself. I'll go into your mom's office and read a book."

"What if the security guards do a check of the house?"

When Tania had first told me about the security guards and their dogs, they sounded frightening enough, but at least then I could assume they were human. Now things were different. What were security guards of the future like? They might be bonecrushing robots. Or they might be great hulking men who had been genetically engineered for the job.

"I love libraries," I said.

The first thing I noticed when we went out of the house was the silence; even though the road was full of traffic, there was no noise. The other odd thing was that the traffic was so orderly. There was no stopping or overtaking. The tiny cars slid along in neat little blocks, all at the same speed.

It was so orderly that it depressed me, and I found myself doing something I'd never done in my life before: I wished I was in the noisy, smelly tangle of traffic at Beckersby Junction on a Saturday morning.

There was a chance that the library we were going to was one I'd been to before, but I didn't recognize my surroundings, and I had no idea what part of town we were in. Everything was pleasant enough to look at, in a monumental kind of way, but it didn't make me feel any better; it all seemed to be pale, massive sweeps of concrete – walls, roads, sidewalks, and buildings – gleaming like ghosts in the dusk. There was an occasional struggling tree.

It was a dream landscape, the sort where you wander around trying to find your lost parents, and it struck me as particularly appropriate to the way I was feeling.

"We'll just walk down here," Tania said, "and then we can get a cab."

We were walking toward a little bay in the sidewalk. A frail shrub scattered blossoms there, and a sign said, "Hail cabs here."

Tania hailed a cab; and I was halfway into the front seat when I jumped out again. "I'm not getting in there."

"What's the matter?"

I couldn't believe she needed to ask. "Look! There's no driver. There's not even a place for a driver."

·"It doesn't need one. It's got a computer."

I tried to explain things to Tania. I wanted her to know that the shock I'd had that day made it extremely hard for me to trust a microchip again. Wasn't that what had got me into this mess?

But just as I was getting into my stride I saw something – a tall figure, with dark hair, disappearing into the space between the buildings. I only saw him for a moment, but I would have recognized that man's figure anywhere.

"Dad!" I yelled. I left Tania standing by the cab and went running after him.

He turned around, peering at me in disbelief. "Mike?" A slow, delighted smile spread over his face. Then he flung his arms wide and caught me in the bear hug I'd missed for so long. "Mike, Mike, you don't know how glad I am to see you."

I thought I had a fair idea. He was probably as glad as I was to see him, which was a whole lot. I hadn't realized till this moment how much I'd missed him.

He held me at arm's length, then pulled me to his chest again. "And your mom?" he said. "How is she?"

"She's okay."

"Really?" Dad seemed to be just a little disappointed. "Not missing me desperately?"

"Not desperately," I said. It came out as "Mmrph," because he was hugging me to his chest again.

During all this Tania had been waiting by the cabstop, and now she came over to join us. "Someone you know?" she asked politely.

I introduced them. They brushed each other's palms in a strangely formal handshake, and Dad thanked her for looking after me.

"We'll see Tania home first," he said, as we turned and walked toward her street, "and then we'll go to Westvale and see about getting ourselves home. You can give me the cable now – I'd feel better if was in my hands."

"Cable?"

"You got my message?" Dad looked at me uncertainly.

"What message?"

"The one I sent you on ..." he tried to remember; "on Sunday night." He ran his hands over his hair, sighing. "No, I suppose you didn't, or you wouldn't be asking."

I pulled a crumpled piece of paper from my pocket. "Is this it? The one that says, (¬__*!7жs2()_{ 421Ñ #{. ø_/-}_ _{|, ~_°8."

"That's the one." A sudden tiredness seemed to come over him, and he stopped, leaning against the wall. "Actually," he said, "it's supposed to say, *Dear Mike, would you or your mother please go to Sundstrom's and get a flat gray ribbon cable with two universal connectors. Put them on top of the black computer, press the TRANSFER button, and when you get the dialogue box saying* DO YOU WISH TO TRANSMIT, *stand well clear and say* "Yes." *And don't ever go near the computer again. It's dangerous. Your loving dad.*"

I said, "It lost a bit in the transmission, Dad."

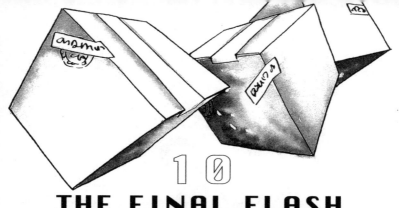

THE FINAL FLASH

We had reached the corner of Tania's street. Now that I looked at it from this end, I could just recognize the street I'd visited a few days earlier. The factories and workshops had gone, and tall concrete houses stood in their place, but the car park still looked familiar. Even though it wasn't a car park anymore – it had been planted all over with trees and bushes – I still recognized the low brick building that stood beside it. On the side wall, in fancy letters, were the words, THE CAR WASH COFFEE SHOP.

"Mr. Alvarado," Tania said, "you don't have to worry about your cable. It's in our computer. I'll give it back to you."

Dad shook his head. "Mike will need it to get home. That's how you came, isn't it? With

Tania's computer, the one from the Beckersby office?"

"Yes, but I can't get back with it, Dad. I've tried. Mom's taken her computer back to work and it's not connected anymore."

He grabbed my arm. "She's *moved* it?"

"I think so. Does that matter?"

Dad patted my arm. "No, no, probably not." But he didn't speak again until we were nearly at Tania's house. He just walked along staring at the ground, one hand behind his back and the other pressed to his forehead, the way he always did when he was thinking. I used to think it was funny until now.

"Is there something wrong?" I asked, but quietly, because I didn't really want an answer.

"The computer shouldn't be moved while someone's using it," Dad said. "Unless you know what you're doing, it's impossible to line it up again. The computer that I used to get here is locked in a shed at the Westvale office, and it'll stay there till I get back – I hope."

I remembered something Mom had said, about the only other Vector 3e waiting for someone to come back from vacation. I said, "Dad, does Mom know where you are?"

Dad sighed. "No. The Directors insisted on telling her I was in Venezuela. They said they didn't want to frighten her by telling her the truth."

"Mom'll frighten *you* if she hears you say that."

"We've got to get home to her first," he said grimly.

We had reached Tania's house. Her parents were still out, so Tania and I sat down on the grass to wait. Dad, with nowhere else to walk, made do with pacing up and down.

"I came here to iron out a few problems with the hardware," he said. "But now I've come across a whole lot more."

He looked at me as he said it, and I knew he meant me.

"Soon after I arrived in this time," he said, "I realized that the computer had a faulty cable. I didn't want to risk using it for the trip home, so I went to the library to find out where the spare computer was – that's the one your mother and Tania have got. I was going to switch the cables.

"But while I was checking through old records I came across a newspaper report. It told the story of a boy called Michael

Alvarado, who was standing by a computer one Monday afternoon when he suddenly disappeared."

He wasn't telling me anything I didn't know, but a distinct creepiness came over me.

"When I read that," said Dad, "I knew which computer it was, and where it was. So I took a long shot and sent you a message. But the cable wasn't up to it, and all you got was garbage."

My mouth felt as if it was full of sand. "Dad," I said, "did you ever find a newspaper report saying the boy had come back again?"

"No," Dad said, "I didn't look."

I didn't blame him for not looking. I'm not sure I would have, either.

Tania said, "Mr. Alvarado, Michael doesn't need our computer to get home, does he? He could go home with you. You can take our cable and put it in your computer, just like you were going to."

"Yes, well," said Dad distractedly, "we'll work something out." But he didn't sound convinced.

Just then Tania's parents came home, arriving in a pale, silent little car that slid in through the gates almost before we noticed it.

But they noticed *us* all right; I don't think they were happy to see their daughter sitting there with a couple of raggedy strangers.

Perhaps that was why they didn't exactly welcome us. Or maybe there was another reason: Tania introduced us as "Mike and his father, Mr. Alvarado," and her father said, "Alvarado. Don't I know that name?" He made it sound as if he'd met an Alvarado once who'd caused him some problems, so I knew it couldn't be us.

Whatever the reason, I could see that they didn't even want to let us into their garden, let alone their house. Tania had to insist, telling them that she had promised us a cup of coffee, before they would let us in.

Tania's mother, a haughty lady with very short, sleek black hair and clothes even baggier than her daughter's, showed us into the little office I'd had been in earlier. The room was so tiny that the five of us only just squeezed in, and I wondered why with such a big house, they didn't invite us into a bigger room. They probably thought that the smaller the room, the less in it for us to steal.

Tania's parents gave us a cup of their thick coffee and talked to Dad and me for awhile in

a meaningless sort of way. I tried to be polite
and join in, but I was disturbed to see that
Dad wasn't saying anything. He just sat staring
into his coffee, and after awhile I had to face
up to the thought that it wasn't just the coffee
that was making him depressed.

"Dad," I whispered, "I can go home with
you, can't I?"

"Not with me," he said quietly. "The two of us can't go home with the same computer. Not without an extra cable. So you'll have to go first, and send a cable back for me. Don't worry, I'll be all right."

I knew he was being noble. I had the feeling that there was still a piece of the puzzle he wasn't telling me, and I was afraid that I mightn't discover it until too late. Maybe there was no way of getting him the cable he needed, and he'd be stuck in the future for ever.

"Do have another cup of coffee," said Tania's mother, fluttering blue and white striped fingernails at us. I knew she meant, "Hurry up and finish your coffee and go."

"Alvarado, Alvarado," muttered Tania's father, wrinkling his forehead. "I've seen that name somewhere." Abruptly, he got up and left the room.

Dad stood up, too. "If you'll allow me, I'd like to –"

There was a silent red flash, and my hair stood on end. In the same instant, I heard a woman's low, triumphant laugh, and something heavy crashed down beside me.

And there was Mom, standing between me and Dad with a bunch of cables as big as a bunch of bananas in her hand.

"Mom!" "Rosie!" Dad and I exclaimed together. "I only wanted one!" Dad said.

"There was a faulty batch. I got a lot, to be safe. If it hadn't been for a faulty cable, Michael would never had been able to activate the POST TRANSFER functions. I wasn't taking any more chances."

Just then Tania's father came back in, carrying two big, dusty cardboard boxes. "Are these yours?" he asked. "There's still another one in the attic. They were here when we moved in; looked like they'd been here forever. I'd have thrown them out if they didn't look so old."

Then Dad explained what had happened, and Tania's parents seemed to thaw a little. They took our coffee cups away, in case we accidentally took them with us, but they said goodbye in a friendly enough way. I said a special goodbye to Tania, and when no one was listening, I promised I'd try to write.

The three of us (and the boxes with our long-lost clothes in them!) got home without mishap, but we didn't arrive where I thought

we would; we turned up at the back of a mover's warehouse.

The first thing I did when we got home was change into some proper clothes; in the garden next door I'd caught the flash of Anita's gold belt, and this time I wanted to be prepared.

But one thing was still puzzling me. That night at bedtime I said to Mom, "How did you know Dad needed a cable, and how did you know where to bring it?"

"It was easy to work out," she said. "When you disappeared, it was obviously the fault of the computer. So I checked the numbers you'd been dialing. There was only one possible one, and that was Tania's. The computer also has an automatic archive: whatever messages come in get compressed and stored. That was how I found Tania's address. I also found Dad's message. I had to use Decode to read it, but at least I got it. Your dad still has a lot of explaining to do, though; I knew that he was on an important assignment, but he'd traveled a lot farther than Venezeula!"

"But why did you move the computer?" I said.

"I had to. If you were going to get home again, the computer had to be in the same place in the past as it would be in the future. At least that was the way that the cable was *meant* to work. So I moved it to 17 Utah Street. That just happens to be where our mover has his warehouse – *and* where our boxes of clothes went, instead of being delivered here."

I drifted off to sleep wondering whether I'd ever enjoy ordinary computer games again. One thing was for sure: after all I'd been through, Shadda and The Last Wizard would seem like child's play!

TITLES IN THE SERIES

SET 9A

Television Drama
Time for Sale
The Shady Deal
The Loch Ness Monster Mystery
Secrets of the Desert

SET 9B

To JJ From CC
Pandora's Box
The Birthday Disaster
The Song of the Mantis
Helping the Hoiho

SET 9C

Glumly
Rupert and the Griffin
The Tree, the Trunk, and the Tuba
Errol the Peril
Cassidy's Magic

SET 9D

Barney
Get a Grip, Pip!
Casey's Case
Dear Future
Strange Meetings

SET 10A

A Battle of Words
The Rainbow Solution
Fortune's Friend
Eureka
It's a Frog's Life

SET 10B

The Cat Burglar of Pethaven Drive
The Matchbox
In Search of the Great Bears
Many Happy Returns
Spider Relatives

SET 10C

Horrible Hank
Brian's Brilliant Career
Fernitickles
It's All in Your Mind,
    James Robert
Wing High, Gooftah

SET 10D

The Week of the Jellyhoppers
Timothy Whuffenpuffen-
    Whippersnapper
Timedetectors
Ryan's Dog Ringo
The Secret of Kiribu Tapu Lagoon